Paradise Island

Paradise Island

A Dreamer's Guide to the
Life Lessons We Learn From
Our Own Human Nature

BRANDON ROYAL

Maven Publishing

Published by:

Maven Publishing
4520 Manilla Road
Calgary, Alberta, Canada T2G 4B7
www.mavenpublishing.com

Library and Archives Canada Cataloguing in Publication:

Royal, Brandon, author
Paradise island : a dreamer's guide to the
life lessons we learn from our own human nature
/ Brandon Royal.

Issued in print and electronic formats.

ISBN 978-1-897393-10-9 (paperback)
ISBN 978-1-897393-12-3 (ebook)

I. Title.

PS8635.O953P54 2007   C813'.6   C2007-905537-0

Cover design: George Foster, Fairfield, Iowa, USA
Mermaid illustrations: Ashley Vercekaites, Calgary, Canada

The cover text was set in Melanie and Minion.
The interior text was set in Scala with section headers
set in Azuki.

*I once had three
dreams about living in
paradise.*

Prologue

Ode to Paradise Island

Blessed are those who have suffered the scourge of shipwreck—those who have swum warm waters and crawled onto these sandy shores—for they shall be rewarded with reprieve on this magnificent isle. Let's remember the world as it once was, when mermaids sang songs to us and saved us from drowning, and pirates greeted us and offered much drink from their barrels and flasks. But let's live to cherish this world as we now find it, where happy-go-lucky bar-goers have no wish to be rescued from the pleasures and vices of their tropical havens. And the mermaids—may they forever be beautiful island maidens who use their feet to dance into the night rather than their tails to frolic in the ocean by day.

DREAM ONE:

I dreamt that
I was part owner
of a bar located
in the midst of
a barhopping
wonderland.
This bar was called
The Lucky Duck
Bar.

The Lucky Duck Bar

One day, a most unusual thing happened. There was a meeting of the Lucky Duck bar owners, and to everyone's surprise, six people each presented an ownership claim to twenty-five percent of the bar. Apparently, the owner, whose share I had purchased, had also sold his ownership percentage three times over. Not surprisingly, a real brouhaha erupted and simmered for some time. As a practical appeasement to all "owners," and with a few concessions pending, it was finally agreed that now there would be six owners, each with a one-sixth ownership.

Unfortunately, with six owners, making simple decisions regarding the bar's operation would, from now on, be far more difficult. Everything had to be voted on in order to be agreed upon. One owner wanted to tile the entrance and install a black metal door while another wanted a brick underlay with a wooden door. Some wanted special discounts on drinks and an extended happy hour. Three of the owners also wanted to directly manage the bar, lending valuable ideas where they saw fit. Although everyone agreed that Mama Palooza and Daddy Doodle should continue to co-manage the bar, the issue that caused the most consternation was the decision on whether to renovate the bar and perhaps join a bar group.

There were seven bar groups in and around Dreams Avenue: Sunset Association, Pooch & Prancers, Margarita Group, Midnight Matadors, Lighthouse Partners, The Grateful Good, and the Tipsy Tattlers. The Lucky Duck was not a member of any of them.

One of Lucky Duck's owners was a man named "Napalm" Tucker. He was a Paradise Island original and a veritable party animal with a penchant for irreverence. Donning a black patch over one eye and a large silver chain around his neck, he needed only a sword to achieve the stature of a real pirate.

The trend on Dreams Avenue was toward bigger, flashier bars that were part of bar group. Napalm didn't believe in joining a bar group. He looked at the bar groups as a scam. Things never worked out the way they were supposed to and owners always lost money. Nor did he believe in the need to renovate. He wanted to keep the character of the bar and cover the walls with paraphernalia and old pictures. One afternoon he showed up to the weekly meeting with a few keepsakes of his own: a lacquered photograph of an inebriated, topless bar girl, a laminated black-and-white picture of a drunken patron pole dancing on stage, and a mounted glass frame honoring a girl's G-string and bra. Napalm also brought a few giveaways, including a batch of newly minted white T-shirts. The design on the front of these shirts was that of a male skeleton dressed in a blue suit and black tie, sitting by himself with one hand resting on a brown park bench. With cobwebs trailing from his skull, the caption read, "Waiting for the perfect woman."

Nevertheless, it was decided by a four-to-two vote that the owners would renovate the Lucky Duck bar, but they would not join a bar group. For two weeks a sign was posted "Closed for Renovations." During this time, Mama Palooza and the girls took a short vacation, although no one could say exactly where they had gone. Then the bar re-opened in glittery fashion and lots of people arrived to check it out. All the bar staff basked in the excitement and the noticeable increase in business. One owner said that the bar had the same energy and glitz of its inaugural opening, just two years before. Another owner was adamant about expansion and even had drafted a business plan for the purpose of soliciting more investors. While some bar owners viewed the spike in business as the new normal, others saw the increase in business as part of an identical cycle that accompanied every bar renovation.

They say that a candle that burns twice as bright burns half as long. Sure enough, after a few weeks, most regulars went back to their favorite bars and business at Lucky Duck returned to its previous level. Who could doubt that many of the folks who showed up at the opening were attracted by drinks at promotional prices, and the chance to win door prizes and enter free raffles?

One afternoon, a couple of bar owners sat squabbling about why no one had renewed the fire insurance policy and why double payment had been made for the electricity surcharge fee. A third owner was sitting off to the side, chatting to me about the bar.

"Making money in bars and having fun are two different things," he said. "I bet the bars you have the most fun at are the ones where the owners are eighty percent trying to have fun and twenty percent trying to make money. As soon as this percentage is reversed—you're eighty percent trying to make money and twenty percent out to have a good time—the enjoyment in the bar falls out. And as soon as you let the bar get big, you're in it to make money."

Margarita Mermaids

I mentioned to him that I didn't mind the sleek look of the refurbished bar, but missed some of the simple touches, including the plaques with clever sayings that used to adorn its walls:

Hangovers: Installed and serviced here.

You can only be young once, but you can be immature forever.

You're not drunk if you can lie on the floor without holding on.

Be careful shooting anything in this bar that isn't moving. It's liable to be the hired help.

And I thought it was a real pity that the wooden sign that hung in front of the bar stools had been removed. On it were scrawled the enigmatic letters: "I. I. T. Y. W. Y. B. M. A. D." First-time bar patrons would stare at the sign and soon query: "Hey, what do those letters stand for?"

"If I tell you, will you buy me a drink?" the bartender would reply.

"Deal," the patron would say. "So tell me what it means."

"I already told you—*If I Tell You, Will You Buy Me A Drink.*"

❤ ❤ ❤

Never while living in the West had I met such interesting characters or encountered folks so willing to share their stories with others they barely knew. I couldn't help thinking how much the bar world was but a miniature version of the world itself. It was as if each bar had its own character and personality, and even mood swings. One night a favorite bar might be busy, the next night quieter. Some moments clicked like lightning caught in a bottle. Other moments were sillier than the duel of the dunces.

Most patrons were friendly, some preachy, others grumbled, and a few hollered. But whether they drank vodka or scotch or beer and schnapps, bar patrons were far more similar by nature than they were different by nurture, and unpredictably so. One had to look no further than the practice of bell-ringing.

Cast in bronze or tempered of steel, the bar bell hung as a permanent fixture in each and every bar. Bells could be the size of a farm bell or as large as a church bell. One pull of its rope handle—"clang, clang, clang"—and everyone in the bar roared. Bar girls swooned. The bell-ringer had bought every girl in the bar a drink, and for the next fifteen minutes he was circled by a gaggle of vixens and treated as if he were the most handsome man in the world.

One afternoon, I was chatting with two of the other bar owners, Mike and Steve, about an epic bell-ringer's showdown. "Let me tell you about bell-ringing," Mike said. "Some local expat named Shorty was in Pharaoh's a few months back at the same time our beloved Titus was there. Titus rang the bell first. I guess the testosterone barometer was high because Shorty took this as some kind of challenge and rang the bell a couple of minutes later. Well, this took some of the polish off Titus' bell ring."

Steve embellished: "A bell-ringer gets to bask in the glory for at least half an hour. You like to have some time for the girls to finish their drinks and engage in a little worship. They parade over to thank you for the drink, give you a kiss on the cheek and all the rest."

"Yeah, but Shorty didn't like this so he rang the bell," Mike continued. "Titus didn't like that and he rang the bell a minute later. Then Shorty rang the bell. The two of them stared each other down throughout the exchange."

"The papasan, Daddy Doodle, and the mamasan, Mama Palooza, were just loving it because they get a small percentage of all the bell rings, too," Steve added. "All the girls in the bar receive fifty cents' commission for each drink, so they were bouncing up and down the entire time."

"Then ten minutes later Shorty rang the bell—again. I guess this was like adding insult to injury. It incensed Titus so he rang it one more time. Then it started up all over again!"

"How long did this go on?" I asked.

"I swear—one-and-a-half hours before it was all over," Mike touted. "The mamasan was walking around like a hen on hot coals, counting and recounting the girls on the floor and the ones left on the dance stage, trying to make sure each girl got the right number of drinks."

"Shit!"

"After ten bell rings each, a total of twenty all together, the papasan approached Shorty and Titus one at a time and told them, 'Thanks gents, but really, no more bell rings—we can't serve any more drinks.'" Then he patted each fellow on the shoulder and that was that.

"I can't imagine any papasan in Paradise Island stopping a customer from ringing the bar bell."

"Almost a *Ripley's Believe It Or Not* entry," Mike said. "Usually the mamasan and girls are itching to find ways to get guys to ring the bell."

"What were the drinks?"

"Standard margaritas."

"How the hell did they pour so many?"

"That's just it. They couldn't. The bartenders kept making drinks and passing them to the waitresses, who themselves lost track. They even had to go next door and borrow mix from their sister bar. Then they ran out of glasses. They also ran out of counter space. Imagine—some bar girls had only finished two of their drinks with eight still on the table and ten more waiting to be delivered. Where could you put twenty drinks with bar counters this wide?" said Mike, gesturing with his hands wide enough apart to measure the tread of a car tire. "Of sixty girls working in the bar, some forty were still on shift and this translated to—let's see—forty girls times twenty drinks per girl—800 glasses!"

"What did it all cost?" I asked.

"Not a king's ransom. About 2,500 to 3,000 dollars. But that's real money here."

Mike continued: "The next day the bar had a new rule. Bell rings would be charged at a flat rate of 150 dollars per ring. This would eliminate the pain of having to count each and every girl whenever the bell was rung."

Ode to the Bar Bell, Ode to a Bell Ring

Bell's a ringin'
Mermaids singin'

Drinks a flowin'
Faces glowin'

Heaps of huggin'
Eyes a lovin'

Kisses oozing
Warm carousing

Then the drinks fade
And I'm alone till then
But what a sweet dream
Till I ring the bar bell again

Siren's Song

♦ ♦ ♦

Oh Lord! Grant me the courage to make this wayward journey, but not the will to resist these mortal temptations. The touch of breezy tropical air…the taste of ice-chilled blended drinks…the cheerful salutes of seasoned bar-goers…the magical hugs of welcoming bar girls.

♦ ♦ ♦

Located behind the Road Warrior bar and Sally's Saloon, the Typhoon Club was housed in a pyramid-shaped building. True to its name, this club's interior resembled a sea-borne storm landing on a tropical beach. Sand was scattered on the bar floor and water funneled behind clear plastic walls. Artificial palm trees planted in the floor arched to resemble trees bending in the wind.

Pandemonium was brewing when I walked though the curtained door late one evening. The bar's theme song had just hit the speakers and the girls dancing on stage had dropped to their hands and knees to shake their heads in sweeping circles, their long hair swirling like pom-poms. Off to the right of the stage I saw a burlesque of erotic dancing and pantomime that was reaching ocean-swell proportions. Two queens of bar antics were using their God-given gifts to terrorize a group of high-rolling bar patrons. In tag-team fashion, one feline took the dancing reins—feet kicking, hands flailing, butt sticking out, all with a big smile and enticing eyes. As she danced, her compatriot bent over the table in front of the men and groaned as if someone was grabbing her from behind. As soon as one of the men stood to reach for her, she would spring up, circle around, and let off a provocative screech to the wild applause of all the other bar girls. These bewildered bar patrons looked like freshwater bass following a shiny lure in ever-widening circles. Then the girls switched routines and the other became the paragon of perpetual dancing motion while the first bent over the table and moaned.

When the theme song of the bar had finished, a few of the bar girls at the back of the bar burst into the Island language, nicknamed "Coco Lingo," joyfully enunciating the lyrics of a perverted bar jingle. Part of the mystique was that they knew that none of the foreign patrons could make sense of the lyrics. The girls still dancing on stage exploded in laughs, shouts, and concocted dance routines.

It was at the Typhoon Club that I first laid eyes on Lovely. From that moment forward, my mind said, "I must have her!" Was it a chemical reaction? Perhaps it was the way her moves spun a hypnotic halo when she took to the stage and lit up the dance floor. Perhaps it was the way her breasts hung like firm peaches or the way her hair caressed the back of her revealing costume.

I was infatuated at the prospect of a good girl turned bad and I was smitten by Lovely's coyness. One moment she purred like a house cat; the next, she hissed like a feral ocelot. When I asked her, in a tone of sexual innuendo, what other patrons liked, her response was, "They like this bar." Indeed, if pleasing looks were the spark plugs that ignited my engine, then a pleasing personality was the piston that kept my motor running.

To me, Lovely was different, but she had one thing in common with the other ladies of Dreams Avenue—the eyes of enchantment. I was convinced that the women of Paradise Island had the nicest eyes I had ever seen. They were warm and inviting—a combination of desire, longing, and vulnerability, with a tad of mystery thrown in. Were these damsels flirtatious! The moving of eyes and eyebrows was a national pastime. Girls sitting at tables with their male friends had no problem getting into the act as long as their "boyfriends" weren't watching. A quick look from her eyes said, "I'm with him, but if circumstances were different I'd be with you." Everybody was getting some and missing more. Smiles and flirtations sent testosterone and estrogen levels jumping like schools of flying fish. In Paradise Island each day unfolded like a world flirting championship, where seductive glances were mandatory, not optional. In a world gone perfect, I envisioned a commemorative postage stamp celebrating *The Eyes of a Dancing Mermaid*.

One week after I met Lovely, I gave her a huge stuffed teddy bear, which I presented to her right inside the Typhoon Club. It sounds a bit crazy. What would a young woman want with a stuffed animal? But Lovely and the other bar girls loved him. They named him Great Bear and anointed him bar mascot. Great Bear was granted permanent sanctuary right behind the bar, and the girls made little white placards for him, which they tied with string and draped around his neck. On these cards were scribed sentimental notes:

"You're like a golden treasure to me."

"Okay, kiss, r u ready? uuum, uuuuu mmmp!!! hope u feel it. i keep u n my heart."

"See you in my dreams tonite."

♥ ♥ ♥

I thought it was unfair that as a result of the renovation many of the former bell-ringers' names had been removed from the walls. Bar tradition mandated that anyone who rang the bar bell got his name etched on the wall along with a small caption of his choosing. It was also an unwritten rule that any bell-ringer would remain a permanent part of a bar's history regardless of whether that bar changed its name or was redecorated. Besides, what bar owner could rightfully judge which bar-loving potentate should have his name removed from the annals of bell-ringing history:

We dumb dumbs rang this bell three times!
Curly, Larry & Moe

I'm a poorer but happier man!
Ernest Liplock

To Karen—*Love Rod*

Happy B-day "Frogman"
from *Daddy Doodle & Mama Palooza*

I asked Napalm what he thought of the renovated bar. "If it ain't broke, don't fix it," he

Poseidon's Ransom

said. "You renovate and business goes up, then down. And when you close for renovations the second time that really means the bar is closed for good. You can't throw renovations at management problems."

For many small reasons, I wasn't having as much fun being part owner of the bar. I considered having been a bar owner a great experience, even though things hadn't turned out exactly as expected. I decided to sell my share to a newcomer for one-third of what I paid and was free of the bar. As the saying goes, "As one door closes, another opens." Now I would have more time to spend with Lovely and her friends.

♥ ♥ ♥

Dreams Avenue was a bar-goers fantasyland. There were large bars, small bars, fancy bars, austere bars, and bars with barely a door. For the next two weeks following my exit from the Lucky Duck, I went on nightly barhops with Lovely and her best friends, Pinkie and Princess. The girls loved to people-watch at the two biggest bars, where the bar girls wore lavish costumes during theme nights. Club Aphrodite was an eye-popping spectacle. Its bar girls paraded velvety blue outfits with thin white belts, black ankle boots, and blue berets. Seeing so many girls wearing cute berets was like hearing a silent alarm calling you to reach out and grab hold. Dry ice frothed from vents built into the wooden dance floor—a floor in which one section moved like an escalator, zigzagging in and around and mimicking the shape of a crazy eight. Dancers disappeared into a "white cloud" before re-emerging, jiving with their siren-black boots and beacon blue head wear.

The next biggest club was aptly nicknamed the "trophy shop." Wearing gold two-piece uniforms with V-backs, Club Pharaoh girls stood like rows of bronze dolls in the front window of a trophy shop, each one waiting to be engraved. Seeing a panorama of sixty Cleopatra look-alikes certainly warranted the creation of two new words. "Fantasmagorical" and "morphenomenal"—these women were indeed fantastical visions who possessed morphologically phenomenal physiques.

On Lovely's birthday, I brought her to Pharaoh's for a free ride in the Chariot. That night, as on any other, as soon as the DJ announced—"Ladies and Gentlemen, your Chariot of Fire"—all eyes would turn to the large curtain at the back of the bar and out would trot eight dancers harnessed by leather straps, pulling forth a chariot. I got a picture of Lovely and three other birthday vixens saluting from the "drivers" seat as the crowd roared, "Happy Birthday." With a goblet in one hand and bullwhip in the other, these ladies partook in the shortest, most magnificent birthday ride of their lives.

After the "glamour" bars, I was glad to get on to the smaller bars, which were more quirky and every bit as welcoming. Walking down the street with three sensational women hanging on my arms, I had to pinch myself. How could I be this lucky? One passer-by commented that each of these three girls was better looking than the next. Maybe that fellow was right! Princess was the tallest, Prissy had the most curves, and Lovely had the longest, shiniest hair. They complemented each other like water, wind, and waves.

To enter the Road Warrior bar was to discover Amazonia—a bar of tall girls, all with long hair. These ladies dressed in fancy red cowboy shirts and faded jeans, complete with lace frills streaming down their outer pant seams. The head waitress wore a sheriff's badge and she alone dressed in black. Strapped to her booze belt were twin bottles of "white courage." I happily avoided "arrest" by honoring her request for me to purchase a tray of Tough-Sweet-Love, better known as tequila shots with salt and lemon.

Craig, the bar owner of Road Warrior, came over with a few drink specials of his own. Additional shots and a stash of drinks ensured that the evening barhop was proclaimed a roaring success before selective memory loss set in. Thank goodness for the ability to crawl as well as walk. And thank God for alcohol. With it, we'll always have something to blame everything else on.

❦ ❦ ❦

What strands of pearly wisdom had I gleaned from these eventful encounters?

I couldn't help but notice that a number of foreigners living in Paradise Island had soured and lost the magic of the place. It was a remarkable transition. Newbies—those first-time visitors to Paradise Island—arrived optimistic, if not ecstatic, as well as good natured, enthusiastic, thoughtful, and usually overly generous. But as they stayed on and the weeks turned into months, they often became jaded, caustic, lethargic, stingy, and culturally chauvinistic. I wondered how could anyone have plenty of alcohol, adequate money, lots of free time, and live in a place filled with delectable mermaids and still not live happily ever after? This was one of those marvelous mysteries of human nature.

*Life's Lesson:
Everything new
grows old. We have
to fight to keep that
edge of newness.*

DREAM TWO:

I dreamt that I was building a home on a sand-drenched, tropical island. This island was called Crab Shell Island.

Crab Shell Island

While strolling past the Sea Serpent's Travel Shop, I saw an advertisement posted in the window:

Own Your Own Island

It's the ultimate symbol of
status and prestige.
It's like owning a castle,
protected by nature's own moat.

Patrol the boundaries of your little kingdom,
for you are lord of all that you survey.
Idyllic! Fall asleep in the sand,
swim naked in the ocean.

Each island is beautiful in its own way,
with its own unique characteristics.
Build your dream getaway,
and christen it with a bouquet of palm trees.

Why not name the island after
your wife, daughter or yourself?

Just imagine.

The dream of living on a remote island—Robinson Crusoe style, with a thatched-roof house shaded by coconut trees—was one I had held since boyhood. I had just been thinking how bustling life in Paradise Island was, how much drinking I had been doing, how distracted I felt having all those naughty "mermaids" frolicking around in the bars, and how sick I was of living at the Trotter's Inn. I wanted a place to call my own. What could be better than actually owning a piece of paradise?

I was looking forward to spending more time with Lovely and this was an even better reason to build an island getaway. Being a familiar face in Paradise Island, I was always greeted by the bar girls with hugs and kisses. When I did meet up with Lovely, she could often smell perfume or find traces of lipstick on my shirt. Stamping down her foot, she would just stare at me and say, "See how you are?" I knew she didn't mean anything by it. It was just drama, as if everything was part of a big play.

I entered the travel shop to gather more information. While buying a whole island was a whimsical idea, a half-hectare beachfront lot on Crab Shell Island could be purchased for a tidy sum. Sole ownership would also avoid the kinds of petty problems that had arisen from multiple ownership of the Lucky Duck bar. There was just one snag. A foreigner couldn't own property in Islandia, the island group of which Paradise Island was a part—only a local person could. Foreigners who married local women put the property in their wives' names even though they put up the money. I figured that after being together for five months, Lovely and I were partners to be.

Needless to say, Lovely was most supportive of the idea to purchase land on Crab Shell Island and couldn't wait to make a first visit. When she heard that a contractor was needed, she immediately suggested that her two brothers come to work on the property. They had some experience in construction and could both easily work for the cost of a single contractor. Since they were family, they could be trusted. A plan was indeed percolating.

Off we went to see the property. Lovely and I flew from Mango Seed City to Tic-Toc Township, took a jetfoil to Pringle Island and boarded a small bus to Golden Sand Beach. We hiked a short way to Bird's Eye Cottages, which was a guest lodge recommended by the Paradise Island travel office. "Checking-in" didn't require showing any

I.D. or completing registration cards. The desk clerk simply said we should let her know when we wanted to check out. The accommodation was certainly basic: no hot water or amenities of any kind, just a hut with a mosquito net.

Lovely heard from the desk clerk that there was only one bar nearby, named the Tree Branch. It was frequented by visitors who had come to dive or snorkel, as well as foreigners who ran the nearby dive shops.

With such simple living, a dearth of people, and an omnipresent ocean breeze, I had found my piece of paradise. We traveled by boat the next day from Golden Sand Beach to Crab Shell Island and returned at early evening. Our two nights spent at Bird's Eye Cottages were surreal. I sunk the back legs of the wooden beach chair deep into the sand and looked right up at the sky. Hearing the sound of waves crashing on the sandy shore while looking at a starry sky, I found myself pondering things I hadn't thought about for some time. Most thoughts didn't go anywhere: What were other people doing?...Why do we spend our lives rushing around in big cities?...With so many places in the world, why do we live in just one place?

Lovely surprised me late that second night by coming to the deserted beach with only her towel on. She opened her towel and lay naked on top of me on the beach chair. I stared at Lovely—her long black hair showcasing her rounded face—her straight white teeth and full lips, always a delight to watch whenever she spoke—and her smooth brown skin, soft to the touch like baking powder. It was as romantic a moment as I had ever known. This is what I had dreamed about. This was my version of paradise.

♥ ♥ ♥

A week passed while on Golden Sand Beach. The purchase of the lot had gone through and Lovely took care of the paper work and money transfer. I left extra money in my local account to use for construction. Cash payments were the only option as small vendors didn't use checks or credit cards. With the arrival of Lovely's brothers, Maelstrom and Mudslide, it was time to put the finishing touches to the plan. I had the renditions of a blueprint. I knew I wanted a beach house with three bedrooms and two bathrooms. But how detailed should the plan be? Maelstrom, the elder brother, suggested they dig a foundation and use it to house the electrical and plumbing. He also wanted to model the design on another house that he and his brother had built for a couple in their village. I could think of no objection. I reasoned that it would be easier for the brothers to build something they had done before rather than attempt something new.

Lovely chose to stay on Golden Sand Beach where she spent part of her day helping an elderly woman sew dresses. Lola was the town matriarch who, in recent years, had enjoyed sewing banners for fiesta time and for local businesses in need of customized banners and table umbrellas. She was a great-grandmother who was still trying to earn money for her family. Her eyesight had become weak and her hands shaky. Lovely agreed to help her and in return she would learn how to sew dresses with Lola's tutoring. I hadn't failed to notice how much the local women of Islandia contributed to their families. They were the real backbone of society. Mothers raised their children. Then, if their children had unwanted pregnancies, or their marriages failed, or they left the village to find work elsewhere, it was the grandmothers who often ended up raising their grandchildren.

Each day Maelstrom, Mudslide and myself made our way by boat to the construction site. My amazement grew as I realized how much

Aquatic Rapture

there was to do on-site. Although I was only supposed to be overseeing the work, I found myself working harder than at any other time in my life. In addition to helping plan each day's work, I was laboring on-site in the hot weather to lend some extra manpower.

Maelstrom came up with what the brothers thought was a great idea: If they were going to go to all the trouble of building one cottage at the front of the lot, then why not build one additional cottage at the back of the lot with an adjoining gazebo. The extra cottage could house friends or family members who would want to visit. I embraced the idea, but insisted that if larger-scale construction was going to take place, then we needed to bring in a local contractor. Also, with more supplies coming to the island, a dock needed to be constructed sooner rather than later. The island was accessible only by sea and the shallow water near the beach meant that all boat trips had to take place during high tide.

Based on a recommendation that I had received earlier from the manager of the travel shop, I made arrangements to hire Mr. Boon Doggle. The number of workers on-site now totaled six because Boon Doggle, the local contractor-for-hire, brought with him both a laborer and a carpenter. I prided myself on my decision to hire Boon Doggle, who certainly seemed to be able to find shortcuts in terms of sourcing materials and supplies. Employing a brick-making machine at the construction site eliminated the need to transport ready-made bricks to the island. With the foundation already reinforced with standard concrete blocks, hollow blocks would now be used on the sides of the house. Light but strong brick was less likely to crack due to natural adjustments in the foundation. Boon Doggle was able to secure cement mix to his exact specifications, owing to a contact he had in a neighboring town. A merchant that he knew there had a small plant and could make regular deliveries by truck.

Not only had the scale of work now increased dramatically, but so had the number of bottlenecks. A new well had to be dug thirty-five feet deep, twice what had been originally planned. Plastic water pipes buried in the cement foundation of the house were leaking because pipe-ends had been connected using a poor quality sealant. Three sections of plywood had to be ripped up to find faults in the electrical wiring. Two extra power generators had to be purchased along with another half-dozen kerosene lamps.

The water basin needed draining to get rid of an unexpected infestation of insects. And for some reason, permission needed to be obtained from the local mayor's office for removal of several coconut trees. As soon as one task was attended to, another popped up. It reminded me of a game I once played where I pounded a plastic mole with a soft mallet only to have another mole rear its head through another hole in the tabletop.

Although the brick-making machine proved convenient, it did use disproportionate amounts of water and electricity. Water was readily available, but electricity was expensive and difficult to bring on-site. There were also quality control issues with the cement mix. Of the twenty bags of cement mix purchased, four had been lost in transit and another half dozen arrived either half full or adulterated with red brick powder.

I had up to now acquiesced to Boon Doggle regarding his purchase requests. But when Boon Doggle mentioned the need to purchase a whole crate of wood varnish at a local hardware closeout sale, I posed a question to Maelstrom.

"Is varnish necessary to protect wood shingles in tropical weather or can we leave the wood roofing as is?"

"Yes," answered Maelstrom.

I was amazed at how many times I had received a yes answer to an either-or question. Was this some kind of linguistic anomaly? Certainly Maelstrom knew how to construct a house given that he had built them before.

Once a week, Boon Doggle and I made the drive from Golden Sand Beach to the local town to pick up supplies and to place additional orders. During our most recent drive, I could have sworn Boon Doggle had lost his bearings and unnecessarily detoured, only to later rejoin the original road. Was there any point exhibiting bewilderment or asking for clarification? Any attempt to do so would surely be met with an oblique response or a "no-problems" smile. I got the impression that every undertaking was unfolding as a spontaneous event. The funny thing was that there was no slipshod planning when it came to lunch. Boon Doggle and the brothers always brought enough food with them or knew exactly how to secure reinforcements. I wondered to myself whether I should have been building a restaurant instead.

One day work extended through to early evening. I decided to spend the night on the island, rather than heading back to Golden Sand

Beach. Boon Doggle and his crew strung their hammocks at the opposite end of the beach from where the brothers and I pitched ours. At two o'clock in the morning I awoke to a strange sound coming from the ground below his hammock. What insects could be making those clicking sounds? Under the flicker of moonlight, I peered down and saw hundreds of crabs along the beach. I scanned the beach to the rough grass beyond—there weren't just a few hundred crabs, there were thousands and thousands of them! I prayed they couldn't climb four feet up the coconut tree to cling to my hammock. I remained silent for an hour, fully aware that the ground below me was moving.

An hour after daybreak I awoke to find not a single crab. Everyone was up, so I wasted no time in posing a query.

"Oh just the seasonal visitors," Boon Doggle gibed.

"How long does it go on for?" I stammered.

"For about three months. They come between midnight and dawn and by morning they're all gone."

I said no more about the incident. Though I was indeed disturbed by this unexpected discovery, I was still lamenting the difficulties involved in

Ocean's Wrath

building my island residence. I remembered the owners of The Lucky Duck complaining about additional expenses when something in the bar broke or simply disappeared. Based on what I originally budgeted to buy the lot and build the house, I was now looking at another half that amount. And because I was now building an additional cottage and a gazebo, I was beginning to wonder if it could be done without costing a fortune.

Later that night while I was at the Tree Branch bar quaffing a few drinks, I chatted to a couple of foreigners who owned dive shops on the beach. One old-timer with streaked red hair sandwiched beneath an Akubra hat was nicknamed Rickshaw. He had been living in Islandia for thirty years and was interested in how I was making out with the house.

"It's hard to not want to buy something," Rickshaw said, commenting on the island purchase. "That's the way foreigners think. In the West we buy land, we own a house. But the beauty of renting here is that you can always walk away."

"You can always resell," I said.

"That you can," Rickshaw replied, "but when you rent something, the landlord has to make sure everything works. When you own something, you have to make sure it works."

I was secretly hoping that Rickshaw could help resolve the dilemma of whether I should press forward or stop construction. But I didn't want to appear too eager, as if I were no longer in control. I surely didn't want to mention anything about the "surprise invasion" because I was feeling a little silly, not realizing that Crab Shell Island might have something to do with crabs.

"Back home," Rickshaw said, "we take for granted that our house has water and that the electricity works. That's not something you can do here. It's just a matter of time before your water supply or generator mysteriously stops working. And guess who's got to pay the locals to get things back on track?"

"I've always thought of property as a good investment," I said.

"Well in the first place, a foreigner can't own property here. And second, we shouldn't use the word investment over here. It should be speculation. I'm *speculating* in a bar. I'm *speculating* in building a house for my wife on her family's land. I'm *speculating* in a restaurant, gas station, bus station, fish farm, poultry farm, rice mill, coconut plantation. Then we'd have a much better idea of what we're getting into."

"It seems that everything is twice as difficult to do here as it is back home."

"And just as expensive in the end. Have you heard the joke, 'What's the easiest way to make a million dollars here?'"

I shook my head.

"Start with two million dollars."

"That's good!"

I shared a funny story of my own with Rickshaw. "The lady at Bird's Eye Cottages wanted to get the rocks out of the water in front of the cottages so the beach would have smooth sand for swimming. She told Lovely that she paid the local kids five cents for each small rock and ten cents for each big rock they removed from the water. The problem was that as the job of rock removal neared completion, the kids started putting other rocks back into the water so the job could continue."

"Yup, sounds about right," Rickshaw said. "The local inspectors check the dates on the fire extinguishers in all the dive shops. When they find cylinders that have expired, they insist that the owners refill them and offer to do it for them for a charge. Most owners say okay, one less thing for them to do. The inspectors take the canisters away, clean them off, and the next day they hand them right back to the owners without having refilled them, but still charging the refill fee!"

"Unbelievable!"

"If the inspectors want to refill my canisters, I take them out to the street and empty the contents in the ditch before handing them over. They smile, knowing that I know the game."

"You have to stay in control," I said.

"Actually we're almost never in control over here. We think we're in control. And the locals like to give us the illusion that we're in control."

"They sure know how to make you feel like you're king."

"That they do. And that's why living here is so addictive. You feel important. It's an ego trip. But it's easy to get sloppy."

"Gotta love the way the locals call you 'Sir.'"

"Especially the pretty ones," Rickshaw said. He raised his hand at a few friends sitting in the corner of the bar, while simultaneously signaling to the waitress for a few more drinks. "If I could count the number of times a foreigner built a house and had the whole family move in..."

"To stay for how long?"

"Until you finally move out of the very house *you* paid to build. The one her family commandeered right from under your nose! Wonder who's in charge when this happens?"

"I have a hard time saying no," I said. "I always feel guilty putting my foot down."

"Saying no is the difficult part—and not feeling like a moron."

I perked up as if some part of this conversation might be the clue I was looking for.

"It's a constant struggle," Rickshaw admitted. "Some guys can't say no and get taken to the cleaners. Others spend their whole time squabbling over prices with the locals."

"The cheap Charlies."

"When people first come over here they spend their time trying to figure out how things work. How the bars work and how the system works. Figuring out how things work is the easy part. Figuring out how not to let this place drive you nuts, that's the hard part. If you can't keep a smile on your face then what's the use of being here?"

My cold beer was kicking in. Rickshaw was on a roll and making a ton of sense.

Moonlight Emollient

"And when I say figure out how the bars work, don't think for a minute that that's the same as figuring out how this place works."

I could see Rickshaw's face turning redder as he no doubt was feeling the jag from his whiskey.

"We have a saying for that too. "On the day thou sayest, 'I understand this place,' it's time to pack thy bags and head to the airport."

I burst out laughing. "Everyone's got their favorite commandments to live by."

"I've never broken any of them myself," Rickshaw sighed, rolling his head in jest and chuckling in self-confession. "But I've fallen for the slow boil."

"How's that?"

"Throw a live frog into a pot of boiling water and the frog will jump out. Put the same frog in warm water and turn the heat up under the pot and the frog will stay in the water and get boiled. We've all got to watch for the slow boil."

Lovely, who had been talking to the bartender in Coco Lingo, turned. "Honey, did you hear that?" she said. "The biggest pearl in the world was found in the ocean here."

"The pearl is in the vault of some private collector," Rickshaw said, confirming that he knew the story.

"Who found it?" I asked.

"A local diver."

"When?"

"1934."

"How big?"

"More than thirteen pounds."

"Come on!"

"The diver gave it to his boss because the boss saved the life of the diver's daughter by buying her some medicine."

"The boss was a foreigner?"

"Yup."

"A foreigner was living over here in 1934!"

"What amazes me," Rickshaw said, "is that you travel to places and there's always some foreigner who's living in some remote spot. Most local people live in the same town where they grew up and hardly ever travel around this country."

"You're going to Ratadome?" the bartender asked, first looking at Lovely before glancing at me.

Rickshaw nodded.

"What's that?" I asked.

"It's an annual cookout and sporting event," Rickshaw said. "Takes place on the other side of the island. A bunch of retirees live up there. There's a few bars. You're welcome to come."

I only needed to look at how excited Lovely was at the prospect of attending a barbecue to know we were going.

"A sports event?" I inquired.

"Ratadome. Dogs and rats," Rickshaw said with a smirk. "Jack Russell Terriers chase rats released from a cage on the beach. The faster a dog catches a rat the better."

"People bet on the races," the barman chimed in.

"It's like bull-riding," Rickshaw continued. "Points depend on how dynamic the chase is. More points are awarded if the rat evades the dog with twists and turns. If a rat manages to make it from the beach to the wooded area, it's free."

"So the dogs are faster than the rats?" I asked.

"Eight out of ten times. Even when the rat makes it to the wooded area it might still get picked off. The rat will start to climb a tree only to have the Jack Russell Terrier scale part way up the tree and snatch the rat in its jaws."

"How long does it last?"

"That's the funny part. Ratadome is not about the rats and dogs, it's about food. Good old Myles. He thought the whole thing up because he wanted to have a cook-off. The rat races only take about an hour to finish. They act as teasers to get everyone to come. Food is big, Texas style. Myles sure loves to barbecue and it brings everyone together. For six dollars you can't beat it. T-bone steaks the size of steering wheels, baked beans simmering in a cauldron and served with a small stainless steel shovel, a wooden salad bowl the size of a wagon wheel, sweet potatoes covered in tinfoil and stacked in a small pyramid."

❧ ❧ ❧

Oh Lord! Grant me the wisdom to navigate this wayward journey, but not the will to resist these simple temptations. The smell of salt-laden seabourne air... the sight of freshly minted tropical drinks... the seasoned salutes of familiar bar-goers... the warm hugs of welcoming bar girls.

❧ ❧ ❧

Rickshaw drove Lovely and me to Ratadome the next morning. We feasted at the barbecue and took in the many attractions. One fellow had a booth displaying the little treasures he had plucked from the sand using a metal detector. Another vendor was selling birdhouses made from painted seashells. The Partner Hooping contest involved each couple standing inside a large hula-hoop. Regardless of how the couples decided to stand or share the space, the task of keeping the hula going brought huge laughs. One music aficionado maintained an amazing collection of vintage records complete with antique record player. Listening to his records at his beach shack gave you the feeling that you were actually in the recording studio, hearing each song being cut for the first time.

Before returning to Golden Sand Beach, we stopped in at the Blue Stripes Tavern. This watering hole enjoyed an intensely loyal customer base and catered almost exclusively to military retirees. Engraved in the oak-knotted front door was the word "Push" with small writing etched right below—"The other push, stupid." Any patron would be reminded of his illiteracy if he instinctively tried to pull the door open instead of pushing it.

I loved eyeing those special things, often wall hangings, that gave a bar its physical character: ornaments, signs, witticisms, photos, news clippings, T-shirts, posters, paintings, and murals. The Blue Stripes Tavern had charm in abundance. Hanging on its side wall, amid an aura of floodlights, stood a life-sized photo of an amazing island woman. She wore no clothes, except for bandoliers strung over each shoulder,

The sign inside the porthole reads:

NO NAME BAR

WARM DRINKS

UGLY WOMEN

BAD SERVICE

WE CHEAT TOURISTS

REGULARS ONLY

Porthole Peeping

which covered her breasts and crisscrossed over her most private parts. Every loop nestled within these two bandoliers held a single large bullet. There she stood—stark naked—poised but alluring, visible under the glow of moonlight, but protected by the cloak of hundreds of copper-cased bullets.

Finding a single vacant table along the side of the bar, we sat down and Lovely began chatting with Rickshaw. I couldn't help overhearing a conversation in progress between two veterans sitting on bar stools: "I'm a retired Marine and my father was a Marine, but he used to say, 'The best thing about being in the Navy is that you always know where you're going to eat and sleep, and when the shit hits the fan you're all in the same mess together.'"

One patron, who had been playing pool, approached the bar counter, and unscrewing his pool cue and reaching for his case, he said, "Well, time to put my weapon to rest."

"Are you slipping or a-sliding?" asked another patron.

Before the first fellow could answer, the second stood up and grabbed half of his pool cue. They strutted over to corner a barmaid sitting on her break. A few patrons yelled "Minnie!"

confirming that she was the recipient of this week's serenade.

Holding pieces of the pool cue as makeshift microphones, the two crooners swayed their hips to and fro, harmonizing the lyrics of a golden oldie.

This diamond ring used to shine so bright
And this diamond ring used to fit just right

Now lying on your table it's so dull tonight
Gathering dust, when you go out at night

So many dreams in this wonderful thing
Don't throw away what our love can bring

When we said our vows it meant everything
Darling, there's still so much hope in this diamond ring

The young barmaid sat paralyzed, blushing and smiling.

"Bravo, encore!" A chorus of cheers continued to reward the sterling ensemble.

❣ ❣ ❣

What sparkling revelations about life had I garnered from my latest adventures in paradise?

I decided that it was now time to return to Paradise Island. I would halt construction and decide later whether to press forward or sell the property as a work-in-progress. Perhaps someone else would embrace the same Robinson Crusoe dream and take over where I was leaving off. I also missed the regular crowd. Lovely had mentioned wanting to go to seamstress school so she could open a dress shop. I was wondrous as to how long it would take her to learn to sew well enough to be able to make dresses of a salable quality, but however long it might take, it was fine with me.

I had also learned an important lesson about "investing" in paradise. It was more difficult and complicated than one could ever imagine. When I saw a house or hotel in some remote location, I would think of it as a minor miracle. I had newfound respect for any foreigner who managed a business on the outskirts of civilization.

I heard a funny story while at the Blue Stripes Tavern. It was an island "fish tale" about a Western businessman and a local fisherman. The Western businessman was on vacation and, by chance, was waiting at the pier of a coastal village when a boat with just one local fisherman docked. Inside the small boat were several large fish. The businessman complimented the fisherman on the quality of his catch and asked how long it took to catch them.

The fisherman replied, "Only a little while."

The businessman then asked why he didn't stay out longer and catch more fish.

The fisherman said that he had enough to support his family's immediate needs.

"But what do you do with the rest of your time?"

"I sleep late, fish a little, play with my kids, take an afternoon nap with my wife, and stroll into the village each and every evening where I sip wine and play guitar with my friends."

The businessman scoffed, "I have a fine college degree and much business experience. I could help you. You should spend more time fishing and buy a bigger boat with the proceeds. With a bigger boat you could catch even more fish and with those proceeds you could buy several boats, and eventually you would have a fleet of fishing boats. Instead of selling your catch to a middleman you would sell directly to the processor, eventually opening your own cannery. You would control production, processing, and distribution. But you would need to leave this small coastal fishing village and move to the city where you would run your expanding enterprise."

The fisherman asked, "But how long would this all take?"

"Fifteen to twenty years," the businessman replied.

"And what then?"

"That's the best part. When the time is right, you announce you are taking the company public and then you sell your stock and make millions."

"Millions! Wow, then what?"

"Then you retire," the businessman said, "move to a small coastal fishing village where you could sleep late, fish a little, play with your kids, take a rest with your wife, and stroll to the village each and every evening where you could drink and play guitar with all your friends."

Maiden's Retreat

Life's Lesson:
There are always
greener pastures.
Sometimes when we
set off in search of
something, life brings
us back to where
we started.

DREAM THREE:

I dreamt that I was living in a village and being worshipped like a tribal chieftain. This village was named Rumnut Village.

Rumnut Village

Lovely, Maelstrom, and Mudslide insisted that I come and stay with them in Rumnut Village before returning to Paradise Island. They told of how their parents and relatives would love to have me as a guest in their small village located in southern Islandia.

I knew I could use a rest and the thought of a whole family taking care of me was music to my ears. Lovely told me that village living was very cheap, because things cost half of what they did in Paradise Island. She also mentioned how quiet the village was. What a rare opportunity, I thought. I could rest and experience the real local island culture. What could be better than living the simple life, while still enjoying the privileges of being a foreigner in paradise?

The first night in Rumnut Village was a blowout. All the family and village neighbors turned out to celebrate my arrival. A full pig was roasted on a spit and the picnic table brimmed with snacks, sauces, rice, local fruits, and soft drinks. Island rum flowed as if a dam had broken. Dirty dancing and revelry erupted as if fiesta had arrived early. I stood at the center of all the attention like a tribal chieftain surrounded by intoxicated worshippers.

The next morning I awoke with a terrible hangover. The island rum that the locals drank was a rough brew. The brothers and other surviving celebrants staggered around with "fish gills" under their eyes. I gestured to Lovely that I would like to pay for the party—for the pig, food, and drinks. She told me it was around 100 dollars.

"Not too expensive," I said, thinking to myself that the pig alone would have normally cost twice that amount.

"I told you honey," Lovely said, "prices are very low in the village."

With the welcoming party over, the activity within the house ground to a halt. What a relief it was to simply sit in a lawn chair at the back of the house and look out over the cropland and rice fields. It was a land of greens, yellows, and browns. How interesting, I thought. In our everyday world, we mix and match colors that don't always work. But whatever color scheme nature chooses, it always looks good. As the perfect end to a wonderfully relaxing day, I also got to sleep early that same evening.

At four o'clock in the morning, I awoke to the sound of the neighbor's rooster crowing, an hour before daybreak. A horrific wake-up call—was this just a sporadic occurrence? I hadn't even noticed this annoyance the night before. Perhaps I was so drunk that I slept through it.

I stayed awake for a couple of hours before finally getting back to sleep. I arrived at the breakfast table late but just in time to hear that Lovely's parents had decided to take me to the beach. They knew I had not had time to enjoy the beach on Crab Shell Island because everyone was so busy with the construction. How I longed for the smell of ocean water and the feeling of sand squished between my toes!

Maelstrom had secured a narrow island bus with roof storage. They loaded several boxes of food and drink on top of the bus, until the vehicle resembled a caterpillar with bumps on its back.

Except for the need to navigate the potholes in the road, getting to the beach went without a hitch. Removing my shoes and placing them next to my large towel, I wasted no time setting off for a much-needed stroll down the beach to flex my leg muscles and massage my feet. The ocean was a magnificent sheet of blue and the tide played its never-ending game of giving some sand before taking some back. Returning an hour later, I found, to my surprise, that my towel now marked the center of beach activity. Smoke mushroomed from the makeshift barbecue pit and sound bellowed from two large speakers attached to a portable karaoke machine. Mudslide was busy chopping several large ice blocks into smaller pieces to line the ice coolers. Even though local beer was cheap, it tasted like cat pee if it wasn't chilled.

I reminded myself that others might have a different idea of how to spend a day at the beach. With no point in trying to lie down and relax, I decided to infuse the current festivities with some friendly competition. I held up a 20-dollar note as a reward to anyone who could sing the best karaoke song. The cash offering was enough incentive for wannabe crooners to swarm the karaoke machine and turn the microphone into a sacred amulet. The idea was for each person to sing one song and pass the microphone. When the first singer chose to sing three songs, to make sure one would be considered his best, the next singer followed with four songs. That set the stage. Any contestant wanting to sing was forced to wrestle the microphone from the clutch of the person singing. I had little choice other than to raffle the money at the end of the day, allowing anyone who had sung a song or merely wanted to sing a song to be eligible for the prize.

Next I tried to organize a tug-of-war for the kids, noting that they had been left out of the singing competition. A prize of two dollars would be given to each member of the winning team.

Getting two teams to square off seemed like a simple first step. But with everyone wanting to be on the winning team, great jockeying was underway. Parents on the sidelines squabbled among themselves about who should be on whose team. Some wanted their children teamed with so-and-so's grandchildren, others wanted their nephews and nieces competing against so-and-so's stepchildren.

Ships that don't sink sometimes float, and the minor miracle of getting two teams to face off did come to pass. However, instead of having two teams pulling at opposite ends of the rope, team members stood along each side of the rope in alternating positions. The two teams looked like two trains passing each other on opposite tracks. As long as one team pulled in one direction and the other team pulled in the opposite direction, in theory, this structure would yield an identical result. As the sayings go: "A polar bear at noon is the same as a black cat at midnight...If two halves equal a whole, then a whole equals two halves."

Oh, the best laid plans of friend and foe! One moment the boisterous competition was orderly and the next it descended into chaos. As soon as one team looked to be winning, opposing team members resorted to wrestling their closest competitors' hands from the rope. To add to the confusion, anyone forced off the rope or who had been tripped quickly dashed back to the center to rejoin the cause. In scarcely a minute, it looked like a rugby match. Who could tell who was winning the tug-of-war when competitors formed a scrum, lost their bearings, and began rotating sideways across the beach?

To finalize the competition, I decided to enter myself and challenge all the kids. In a fever pitch of hoots and hollers, the parents signaled for the kids to grab hold for the chance of a lifetime. Standing alone at one end of the rope, I stared across at some three-dozen child warriors. Feeling how taut the rope was, I felt like Gulliver awakening to find himself tied down in the Land of the Lilliputians. I pulled hard on the rope, but my feet barely held on the hot sand. Sweat trickled off my forehead, as if I were tugging on a slab of concrete. When they pulled me across

Blue Embrace

the centerline in less than a minute, the parents roared and the kids screeched and leaped with joy. Gasping for air, I was left wondering how these little tots had organized themselves so efficiently to win the tug-of-war and snatch their prizes from thin air.

I later asked Lovely's parents if I could pay them for the outing. Her father said that he thought it cost around eighty dollars. This was still cheap given how many people were involved in the "beach production." The father thanked me and asked me to stay longer.

"You must learn about our culture," he said.

I nodded and smiled in a gesture of courtesy. It was interesting how other locals had also used these same words. Perhaps it was just pleasantry, a thing that the elderly island folk said to foreigners. On the other hand, what if I stayed in the village and became completely fluent in Coco Lingo. What if I learned so much about local culture that I spoke, acted, and thought just like a local? I was having trouble seeing the advantage of trying to become a local if I was and always would be a foreigner.

When I later told Lovely that I had agreed to pay eighty dollars to her father, she added, "Plus ten dollars for fuel." I was not about to get involved in petty family politics, but I couldn't help mentioning to Lovely that earlier that morning I had already given money to Mudslide. Aside from the purchase of tinfoil, charcoal, and lighter fluid, I believed that the change from my large note must have been used to pay for gasoline. When Lovely asked Mudslide about the money, he said he had not paid for gasoline. He instead used the leftover money to buy a new beach chair for me, which the brothers had not unloaded off the top of the island bus because it seemed that everyone was content to stand during the beach activities. Naturally I couldn't take the chair with me upon returning to Paradise Island, so I nodded to the brothers to indicate that they should have it.

By midday I was at the fish market to buy the catch that would commemorate my visit. With no fewer than a half-dozen well-wishers constantly by my side, I was acutely aware of just how precious those solitary moments had been at Golden Sand Beach. I bought the biggest fish I could find—a swordfish! It was as big as the ones I had seen mounted on walls in the taverns and bars. I figured it was important to go out in style. Curious onlookers converged on the fish vendor's stall, staring, gawking, and gasping at the size of the mighty fish.

"Cut?" the vendor bleated, his machete bobbing in the air.

"Whole," I bellowed, shaking my head and raising my clenched fists skyward. Watching family members struggling to haul this slippery mammoth out of the wet market was for me a moment of reckoning. I felt I had earned this feeling of twisted satisfaction.

I now realized that living in Rumnut Village was anything but inexpensive. On a per person basis, everything was cheap, but there was always so much to buy because there were so many people to transport, feed, and entertain. I wondered for a moment what would have happened if I had completed the Crab Shell Island project and everyone arrived to live for months at a time.

The time to leave had come at last. Everyone escorted Lovely and me back to the small airport on the outskirts of Rumnut Village. Her family members were teary-eyed at the prospect of the two of us leaving. I knew that the family meant well and that Lovely and I would laugh about everything later, but when we reached the check-in gate, climbed the stairs of the aircraft, and felt the plane lift off, I did feel a little like a caged dog who had once again been set free to roam the countryside.

♦ ♦ ♦

Oh Lord! Grant me the strength to survive this wayward journey, but not the will to resist these earthly temptations. The smell of flower-scented tropical air...the sound of ice cubes swirling in blended drinks...the festive salutes of seasoned bar-goers...the magical winks of welcoming bar girls.

♦ ♦ ♦

Back in Paradise Island, the days of fun-filled partying flowed together. An early afternoon beer would turn into a late afternoon cocktail. An early evening barhop would turn into an all-evening drink fest. One bar patron would buy a round of drinks and another would willingly reciprocate. And just as you would be thinking of leaving, an owner or papasan would step up and buy a round of drinks for everyone. The situation was as easy to control as floodwater from a flash storm. Local patrons liked to joke that they were so busy doing nothing. Alcohol, island maidens, and camaraderie—yes, these indeed were the three pleasures and three vices of Paradise Island. A regular bar-goer named Party Pete had a wonderful way of describing the endless sightings of beautiful women and the speed with which days passed. "Oh, it goes on and on like an air-raid siren," he'd say. "And the days of our lives go by like picket fences at a drag strip."

I had moved from the Trotter's Inn to the White Orchid Hotel, which had a large swimming pool. Now I had a substitute for the beach as well as a terrific venue to accommodate those stopping by on hotter days. This particular afternoon I needed a nap. Finding the hotel room cool and the pillow soft, I quickly dozed off. I dreamed that I was having a dream. In this deepest but briefest of dreams, I had returned to a day when the earth opened and the sky was filled with dust from a volcanic explosion. I was wading through gray sand like a child playing in a snowfall. Sirens sounded in the streets and locals carried cloth-covered buckets of rice over their heads. Clouds of black smoke shot up from the earth and the weight of falling debris crushed the roofs of houses and bars.

Soaring high into the sky, I could see the bars illuminated as if by the glow of searchlights. They were all changing names, renovating themselves and collapsing under the weight of the volcanic ash, only to rise again as new bars with lights and glitter shining through gray dust clouds. A huge chess game was in progress in the middle of a large field. Elegantly dressed bar girls stood like gargantuan chess pieces: half wore white uniforms, the other half wore black. Each girl had braided hair with small flashing lights attached like decorations adorning a New Year's bash. As soon as a girl was selected for a move, her square lit up and she began to dance. Then clever sayings of the bar world flashed all around the perimeter, as if embedded in the ground. I peered down and saw, "Lucky is he who finds paradise. Luckier still is he who can leave it."

I looked around for the last time in this strangest of moments. It was day but it looked like night. Gray ash fell from the sky like the backwash of a lunar landing. Dreams Avenue, the mother of all hornet's nests, was on fire, and nature was pelting her with big rocks. My earthly paradise had come to an end.

♥ ♥ ♥

I awoke from this dream within a dream. I was startled but relieved that all was fine. I chose to have an early evening beer in quiet celebration at my favorite drink-and-spy perch—Bananitas bar. How I loved sitting behind those mesh front windows, perched on a bar stool with arms resting on the front ledge. With a drink by my side I could take in the sights, sounds, and smells of the street and watch people pass within a foot of my face. Bananitas was located right at the very center of Dreams Avenue. The sidewalk directly in front of the bar bustled with activity and swirled in cacophony—vendors touting, two-bit hustlers pestering, patrons catcalling, drivers bellowing, vehicles braking, horns sounding, and engines revving.

I reflected on how far I had come during the past year and the new life I had made for myself. The regular bar patrons were loads of laughs. Lovely and her friends were a lovable lot—full of energy and fit for forgivable acts of mischief. I had grown accustomed to life's little luxuries: manicures and pedicures, shoulder and back massages, constant hugs, and cheerful hellos.

As much as I treasured my feeling of independence, I admired the way the locals dedicated themselves to their families. Brothers and sisters shared their belongings and friends "lent" and "borrowed" with the regularity of goods changing hands at a swap meet.

I wanted to remain optimistic, to keep up a good attitude, and not get involved in petty politics. I had seen foreigners fall out with one another for the silliest of reasons, and others become so miserable that they had lost the fun of the place. I vowed to never let this happen

Neptune's Harvest

to me. When it came to Lovely, I wouldn't let small financial annoyances involving her or her family ruin our wonderful relationship. I would remember the words she told me when we first met: "A genuine love cares without condition, gives without hesitation, and understands without explanation."

Just the day before, I had run into Captain Cahoots, a local mariner. He had given me exuberant accounts of his chartered expeditions to find giant clams off the northern tip of Cape Bluehorn. When I told the Captain that I wanted to celebrate my one-year anniversary in Paradise Island and was interested in chartering a boat, the Captain also mentioned that he was looking to have a partner join his new business for a minimal investment.

"I harvest giant clamshells," he said. "All that's needed is a boat and dive equipment."

"A boat?" I queried, with eyes that must have sparkled as I envisioned gigantic clamshells that could yield a small fortune back in the West, or "Big Land" as some folks liked to say.

"And large enough to actually live on," the Captain added. "Your Lovely could serve as captain and her friends could join her whenever they wanted."

I said to myself: Just when I had given up on the idea of finding the near perfect investment, along comes this opportunity. A sailing vessel and diving gear—what could go wrong with a business as simple as this?

❤ ❤ ❤

What glittering insights had I sifted from my latest encounters?

The prospect of an ocean breeze and a wooden sailing ship navigating blue water stirred my imagination. Once again I recalled the dream of my early youth:

Galleon ships and buckets of gold

Uncharted South Sea Islands

Mystical women with welcoming smiles

I now understood these thoughts to be nothing more than the desire for wealth, adventure, and love. In Paradise Island, I had found all these things and yet none of these exact things. The wealth I found was marked by the interesting characters met and experiences gained, not by any gold nuggets or jeweled trinkets uncovered. The adventure I found was as much about self-enlightenment as it was about deciphering cultural riddles. The love I found was as much about companionship as it was about romantic interludes.

In the background, I heard bar music and the lyrics of an old song with words sung so strong. It told the story of a "soldier of fortune"—a man who had found love but was growing older, and the songs that he had sung now echoed in the distance like the sound of a windmill going around. How I liked the way the singer's voice reverberated on the word "round." I couldn't get that sound out of my mind. It was the voice of a windmill spinning round.

I remembered the sunsets that Lovely and I shared when living on Golden Sand Beach. The vibrant hues of orange and red were unlike any colors I had ever seen in a photograph. A picture could never capture the breezy air, the sight of the sky changing color in the afterglow, or the feeling of mutual gratitude that came when watching a sunset together. And what good is anything if you can't share it? I always treasured that moment when, without a cloud in the sky, the sun seemed to touch the earth. For a few magic moments, a fireball would sit on the horizon and salute in all its glory. Then a minute later it would drop below the line of sight. You couldn't help wanting a "replay," knowing that for today it had gone.

Watching a sunset always brings a feeling of awe and a moment of sadness. It's strange how the two feelings occur right next to each other. The most spectacular part of the sunset occurs just before the sun disappears. That must be part of the bargain. If we want to experience a complete sunset—the very best part of the sunset—we have to be willing to let the sun go down.

Life's Lesson:
We have to accept
the bad with the
good. It is life's
"imperfections" that
makes the journey
of life interesting.

About the Author

Brandon Royal is an award-winning writer whose educational authorship includes *The Little Blue Reasoning Book, The Little Red Writing Book, The Little Gold Grammar Book,* and *The Little Green Math Book.* During his tenure working in Hong Kong for US-based Kaplan Educational Centers—a Washington Post subsidiary and the largest test-preparation organization in the world—Brandon honed his theories of teaching and education and developed a set of key learning "principles" to help define the basics of writing, grammar, math, and reasoning.

A Canadian by birth and graduate of the University of Chicago's Booth School of Business, his interest in writing began after completing fiction and scriptwriting courses at Harvard University. Since then he has authored a dozen books and reviews of his books have appeared in *Time Asia* magazine, *Publishers Weekly, Library Journal of America, Midwest Book Review, The Asian Review of Books, Choice Reviews Online, Asia Times Online,* and About.com.

Brandon is a five-time winner of the International Book Awards, a seven-time gold medalist at the President's Book Awards, as well as recipient of the "Educational Book of the Year" award as presented by the Book Publishers Association of Alberta. He has also been a winner or finalist at the Ben Franklin Book Awards, the Global eBook Awards, the Beverly Hills Book Awards, the IPPY Awards, the USA Book News "Best Book Awards," and the *Foreword* magazine Book of the Year Awards. He continues to write and publish in the belief that there will always be a place for books that inspire, enlighten, and enrich.

To contact the author:
E-mail: contact@brandonroyal.com
Web site: www.brandonroyal.com

Books by Brandon Royal

The Little Blue Reasoning Book:
  50 Powerful Principles for Clear and Effective Thinking

The Little Red Writing Book:
  20 Powerful Principles for Clear and Effective Writing

The Little Gold Grammar Book:
  40 Powerful Rules for Clear and Correct Writing

The Little Red Writing Book Deluxe Edition:
  Two Winning Books in One, Writing plus Grammar

The Little Green Math Book:
  *30 Powerful Principles for Building Math and Numeracy
  Skills*

The Little Purple Probability Book:
  Master the Thinking Skills to Succeed in Basic Probability

Ace the GMAT:
  Master the GMAT in 40 Days

Dancing for Your Life:
  *The True Story of Maria de la Torre and Her Secret Life
  in a Hong Kong Go-Go Bar*

The Map Maker:
  *An Illustrated Short Story About How Each of Us Sees the
  World Differently and Why Objectivity is Just an Illusion*

Paradise Island:
  *A Dreamer's Guide to the Life Lessons We Learn
  From Our Own Human Nature*